TWINDERGARTEN

Story by **Nikki Ehrlich**   Pictures by **Zoey Abbott**

HARPER

An Imprint of HarperCollinsPublishers

For Max and Zach,
my absolutely positively biggest inspirations.
I love you so much. —N.E.

For August and Olive —Z.A.

This is Dax.

This is Zoe.

They go together like peanut butter and jelly.

On the night before school, the twins had the jitters. The just-about-to-start-school jitters.

Tomorrow, they'd be in different classrooms. And they **absolutely** couldn't imagine what that would feel like.

The twins took out the pins and name tags their teachers had sent them.
Zoe would be with the Awesome Alligators. Dax would be with the Cool Cats.
But what they *absolutely positively* wanted was to be together.

"Being in different classes will give you the chance to make your own new friends," said their mom.

Zoe wasn't so sure.

And Dax **absolutely**

positively

definitely wasn't so sure.

That night, Dax pushed his bed closer to Zoe's.

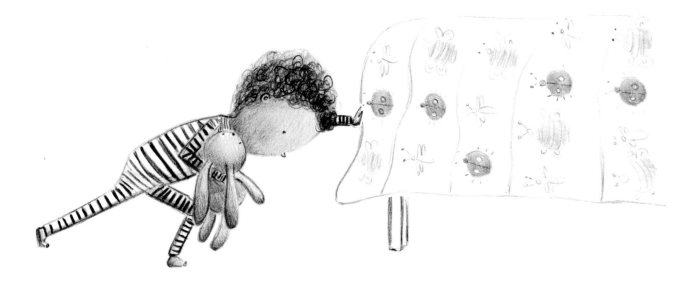

Zoe moved her pillow closer to Dax's and took his hand. It was what she always did when she knew her brother was worried.

The next morning, the twins were up with the sun.
"It's here!" cried Zoe. "Our first day of school!"

In front of the school,
teachers were holding signs.

AWESOME
ALLIGATORS

"Dax! The Cool Cats!" Zoe said.
"And look! The Awesome Alligators!"
Dax smiled. Right away he felt he was
going to like his teacher.

Zoe tried to smile. Uh-oh. Something suddenly felt funny in her tummy.

Dax kissed his parents good-bye and let go of Zoe's hand. "Don't worry,"
he said bravely. "I think we're going to have an **absolutely positively** awesome day."
This time . . . Zoe wasn't so sure.

Mr. Green knelt on the ground. "Hi, Zoe! It's nice to meet you. You're going to have a great time in my class this year."

Just then, Zoe noticed a girl had the same backpack. "I like your backpack!"
"Thanks! I'm Sydney. Did you know it has a secret pocket?"

In the Cool Cats room, Dax started to realize . . . kindergarten WAS cool!
He sang about the days of the week in circle time and built his skyscraper
with blocks during free play.

At music time, Dax met a new friend. "What's your name? I'm Max."

"I'm Dax! Hey, our names rhyme!"

In art class, Ms. Williams noticed Dax working hard on something.

But across the hall, Zoe still felt anxious. She missed
Dax more than she'd thought she would.
She didn't want to cry. But she felt like she might.

At last! Recess.

And there were Dax and Zoe. Back together like peanut butter and jelly.

They climbed the monkey bars and had a contest to see who could swing high, higher, highest.

Recess was the best! But then Mr. Green
blew the whistle.
And just like that, recess was over.
"Bye, Dax," said Zoe.
"Bye, Zoe," said Dax.

As they hugged good-bye, Dax slipped something in her pocket.

"Do you wish Dax was in your class?" asked Sydney as they walked back to the classroom.

"Yeah, kind of," said Zoe. "But at least he's just across the hall."

That's when Zoe remembered the piece of paper in her pocket.

As Zoe was hanging Dax's picture on the name tree, Sydney walked over. She had the class guinea pig in her hands. "We're going to feed Fluffy. Want to help us?"

"Sure!"

Maybe, she realized . . .

kindergarten would turn out to be *absolutely positively* **awesome** after all.